UP, UP, AND AWAY

Margaret Hillert

Illustrated by Robert Masheris

MODERN CURRICULUM PRESS

Library of Congress Cataloging in Publication Data

Hillert, Margaret.
  Up, up, and away.

  SUMMARY: Two children travel to the moon in a
spaceship, do some exploring, and come back home again.
  [1. Space flight to the moon—Fiction. 2. Moon—
Exploration—Fiction] I. Masheris, Robert.
II. Title.
PZ7.H558Up [E] 80–21403
ISBN 0-8136-5596-X (Paperback)
ISBN 0-8136-5096-8 (Hardbound)

        14 15 16 17 18 19 20   02 01 00

Look at this.
Here is something big.
What is it?
What can it do?

It can go up.
It can go up, up, up.
It can go up, up, and away.
And we can go up in it!

What fun!
What fun!
We will go up in it.
We will go away, away.

Come here.
Come here.
Here is a little car.
It will take us up to
where we want to go.

Here we are.
Get out. Get out
and go in here.
Here is where we go.

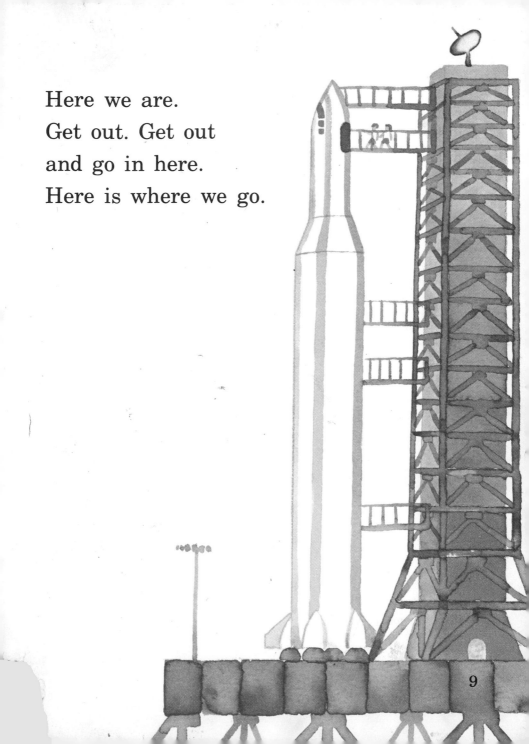

9

Now do this.
We have to do this.
It is good to do.
It will help us.

And away we go!

Here we go.
Up, up, and away to see
what we can see.

12

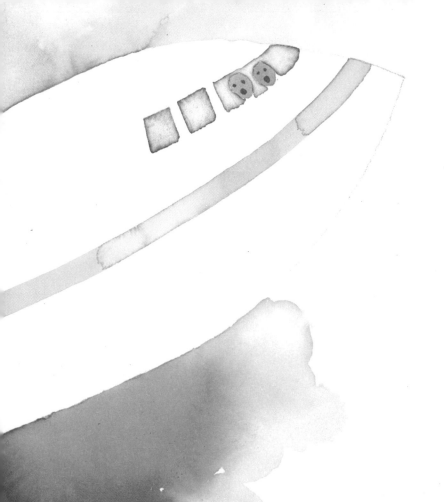

Oh, oh, oh!
What a ride this is!
What a good, good ride!

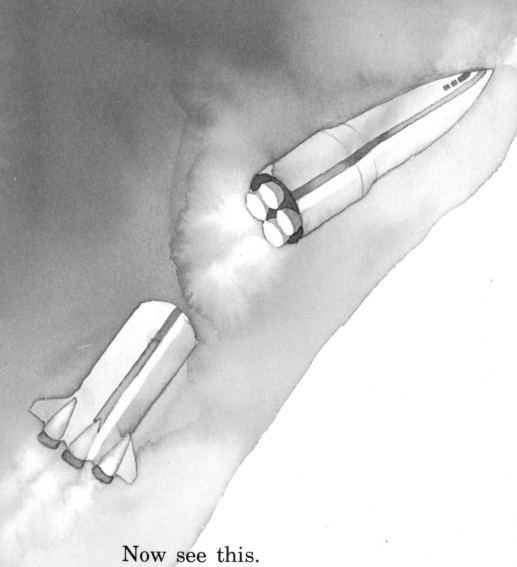

Now see this.
Something will go down,
but we will go on and on.

This one will go down, too.
But we are up here,
and we will go and go.

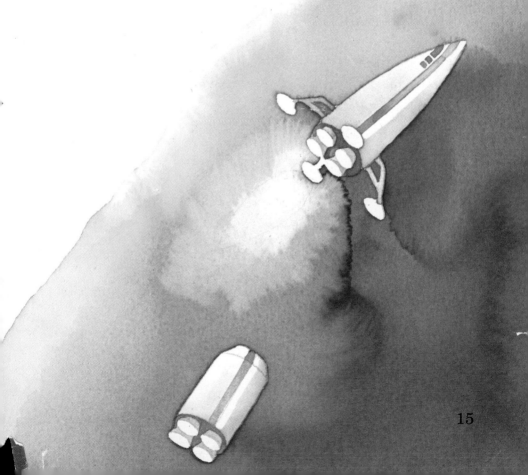

Look out here.
Look, look.
Look what I see.
Do you see that?

16

And now look here.
That is where we want to go.
We want to see what it
looks like.

Here we are.
Oh, here we are.
We will go down, down.
We will get out.
We will find out what
is here.

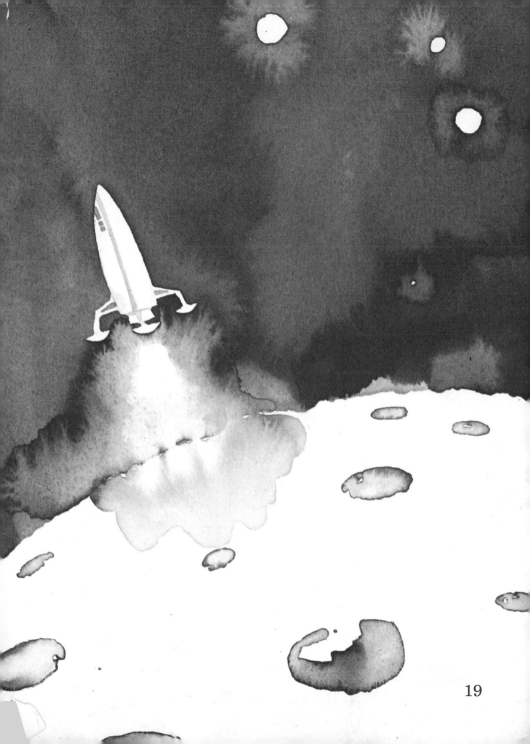

Oh, what big jumps!
What big jumps we can
take up here!
This is fun.

Get into this little car.
Now we will take a ride
to see what we can see.

Look here. Look here.
Down, down we go.
Way down in here.

And now look.
Up, up we go.
Way up here.

Look what we can see.

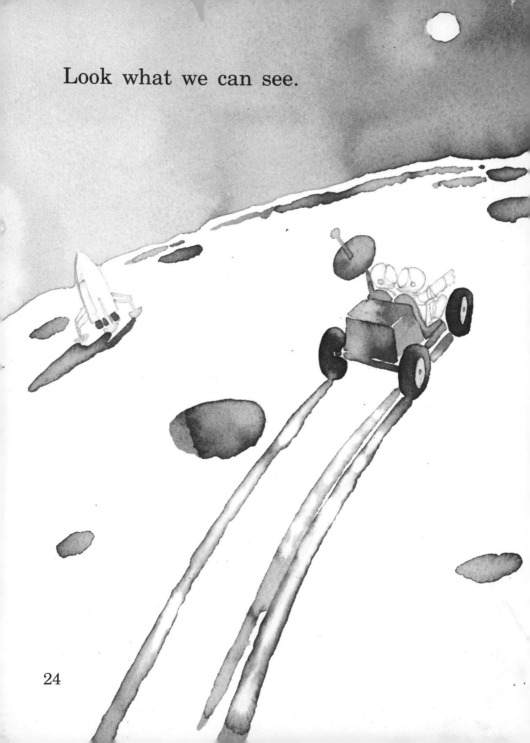

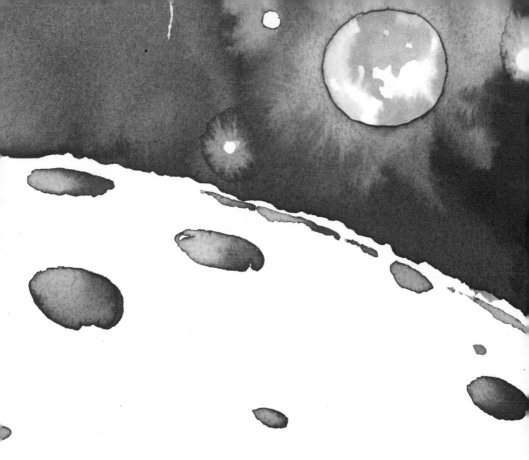

I guess I want to go now.
I want to see my house.
I want to see my mother
and father.
Do you want to go, too?

Get in. Get in.
We will go away now.

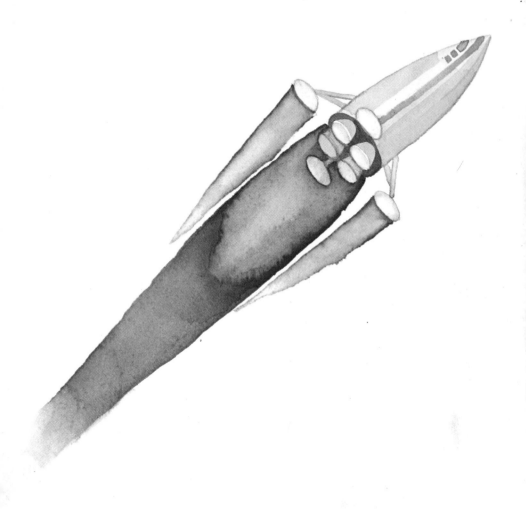

Down we go.
Down, down, down.
Here we come to a good spot.
This is a good spot for us.

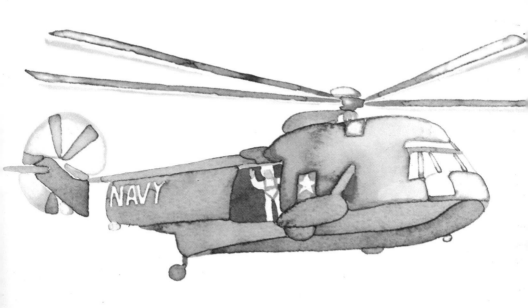

We are down now.
See the boat.
Here comes a boat.
It will get us.
That is good.

31

Margaret Hillert, author of several books in the MCP Beginning-To-Read Series, is a writer, poet, and teacher.

Up, Up, and Away uses the 60 words listed below.

a	get	mother	up
and	go	my	us
are	good		
at	guess	now	want
away			way
	have	oh	we
big	help	on	what
boat	here	one	where
but	house	out	will
can	I	ride	you
car	in		
come(s)	into	see	
	is	something	
do	it	spot	
down			
	jumps	take	
father		the	
find	like	this	
for	little	that	
fun	look(s)	to	
		too	

1.0

DATE DUE